Ladybird  Readers

Pom Pom
is Grumpy

Series Editor: Sorrel Pitts
Text adapted by R J Corrall

LADYBIRD BOOKS

UK | USA | Canada | Ireland | Australia
India | New Zealand | South Africa

Ladybird Books is part of the Penguin Random House group of companies
whose addresses can be found at global.penguinrandomhouse.com.
www.penguin.co.uk   www.puffin.co.uk   www.ladybird.co.uk

Text adapted from 'Pom Pom Gets the Grumps'
first published by Puffin Books 2015
This version published by Ladybird Books 2019
001

Text and illustrations copyright © Sophy Henn, 2019

Printed in China

A CIP catalogue record for this book is available from the British Library

ISBN: 978-0-241-35794-1

All correspondence to:
Ladybird Books
Penguin Random House Children's
80 Strand, London WC2R 0RL

MIX
Paper from
responsible sources
FSC® C018179

Ladybird Readers

Pom Pom
is Grumpy

oharcr2

Based on
Pom Pom Gets the Grumps
by Sophy Henn

Picture words

Pom Pom

baby
brother

Mommy   Buddy   Scout

wake up

playground

jump rope

grumpy

shout

One morning, Pom Pom
wakes up, and he is grumpy.

"Humph!" he says.

He wants his favorite toy,
but he cannot find it.

He looks under his bed . . .

and he looks in his toy box.

Then, Pom Pom sees his baby brother. The baby is playing with Pom Pom's toy!

"Humph!" says Pom Pom.
"That's MY toy!"

At breakfast, Pom Pom's mommy is listening to the radio. Pom Pom does not like the music.

"Humph!" he says. "I don't like that music."

They go to school, but
the sun is too hot.

"Humph!" says Pom Pom.
"It's too hot!"

At school, Pom Pom's friends
are in the playground.

Pom Pom does not play.
He is too grumpy!

"Let's play football,"
says Buddy.

"No!" says Pom Pom.

"Let's jump rope,"
says Scout.

"No!" says Pom Pom.

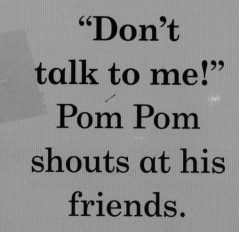

"Don't talk to me!" Pom Pom shouts at his friends.

21

Pom Pom's friends go.

Now, Pom Pom is not grumpy.
He is sad.

"I'm sorry,"
says Pom Pom.

"That's OK," say his friends.
"We have grumpy days, too.
Let's play!"

Now, Pom Pom is not grumpy,
and he is not sad.

He is happy!

Activities

The key below describes the skills practiced in each activity.

Spelling and writing

Reading

Speaking

? Critical thinking

Preparation for the Cambridge Young Learners exams

1 **Circle the correct sentences.**

1 

  a This is Pom Pom's baby brother.

  b This is Pom Pom.

2 

  a This is Pom Pom.

  b This is Mommy.

3 

  a Pom Pom is in the playground.

  b Pom Pom plays football.

4 

  a Pom Pom wakes up.

  b Pom Pom shouts.

Look and read. Write *yes* or *no*.

One morning, Pom Pom wakes up, and he is grumpy.

"Humph!" he says.

1 It is morning. ...... yes ......

2 Pom Pom wakes up. ....

3 Pom Pom is very happy. ....

4 Pom Pom says,
"Good morning!" ....

5 Pom Pom says, "Humph!" ....

3 **Ask and answer the questions with a friend.** 🗨

He wants his favorite toy, but he cannot find it.

He looks under his bed . . .

and he looks in his toy box.

8

9

1

> *What does Pom Pom want?*

> *Pom Pom wants his favorite toy.*

2 Can Pom Pom find his favorite toy?

3 Where does Pom Pom look for his favorite toy?

4 Circle the correct words.

Then, Pom Pom sees his baby brother. The baby is playing with Pom Pom's toy!

"Humph!" says Pom Pom. "That's MY toy!"

10

11

1 Pom Pom sees his **mommy. /
baby brother.**

2 The baby is **looking at /
playing with** Pom Pom's toy!

3 Pom Pom says, "Humph! That's
MY **toy!" / brother!"**

4 Pom Pom **is / is not** happy.

5 **Choose the correct words, and write them on the lines.**

At breakfast, Pom Pom's mommy is listening to the radio. Pom Pom does not like the music.

"Humph!" he says. "I don't like that music."

12   13

---

breakfast   music   like   listening

---

1 It is ___breakfast___ .

2 Pom Pom's mommy is ___listening___ to the radio.

3 Pom Pom does not like the ___music___ .

4 Pom Pom says, "Humph! I don't ___like___ that music."

6 Read the text. Choose the correct words and write them next to 1—4.

They go to school, but the sun is too hot.

"Humph!" says Pom Pom. "It's too hot!"

14

15

1 going	goes	go
2 too	two	to
3 has	are	is
4 It	It's	Is

They ¹ _go_ to school. But the sun is ² _too_ hot. Pom Pom ³ _is_ not happy. He says, " ⁴ _Its_ too hot!"

34

7 **Look at the picture.**
Circle the correct words.

At school, Pom Pom's friends are in the playground.

Pom Pom does not play. He is too grumpy!

1 Pom Pom is at

   a school.   **b** home.

2 Pom Pom's . . . are in the playground.

   a baby brother   **b** friends

3 Pom Pom does not

   a listen.   **b** play.

4 Pom Pom is too

   a grumpy!   **b** happy!

8 Look at the pictures.
Put a or a in the boxes.

1  This is Pom Pom.

2  This is Scout.

3  This is Buddy.

4  These are
Pom Pom's friends.

9 **Look at the picture and read the questions. Write the answers.** 📖 ✏️ ⭐

"Let's play football," says Buddy.

"No!" says Pom Pom.

"Let's jump rope," says Scout.

"No!" says Pom Pom.

1 Where is Pom Pom?

Pom Pom is in the _playground_ ✓

2 What does Buddy have?

Buddy has a _football_.

3 What does Scout have?

Scout has a _skiping rope_.

10 **Look at the picture.**
Write *T* (true) or *F* (false).

"Don't talk to me!" Pom Pom shouts at his friends.

20   21

1 Pom Pom's friends
shout at him.

F

2 Pom Pom shouts at
his friends.

T

3 "I'm grumpy!"
Pom Pom shouts.

F

4 "Don't talk to me!"
Pom Pom shouts.

T

11 **Look at the picture and the letters. Write the words.** 📖 ✏️ ✦

Pom Pom's friends go.

Now, Pom Pom is not grumpy.
He is sad.

22   23

1 (o m P m P o)

Here is ___Pom Pom___.

2 (d i e n f r s)

Pom Pom's ___friends___ go.

3 (r y p m u g)

Now, Pom Pom is not ___grumpy___.

4 (a d s)

Now, Pom Pom is ___sad___.

12 Find the words.

j n o d s o r r y n o u f

s o r r y n f i f r i e n d s h o i s a d n e j i g r u m p y h v b u d a y s m g r d p l a y

sorry

friends

sad

grumpy

days

play

13 **Order the sentences. Write 1—5.**

_5_ "That's OK," say Pom Pom's friends.

_4_ Pom Pom is happy!

_3_ Now, Pom Pom is not grumpy.

_2_ Pom Pom's friends say, "We have grumpy days, too."

_1_ "I'm sorry," says Pom Pom.

14 **Look at the picture.**
Write the correct sentences.

Now, Pom Pom is not grumpy, and he is not sad.   He is happy!

26   27

1 is   Now,   grumpy   Pom Pom   not   .

Now, Pom Pom is not grumpy.

2 is   sad   not   Pom Pom   Now,   .

now Pom Pom is not sad.

3 Pom Pom   Now,   happy   is   !

now pom pom is happy !

15 **Talk about the two pictures with a friend. How are they different? Use the words in the box.**

"I'm sorry," says Pom Pom.

"That's OK," say his friends. "We have grumpy days, too. Let's play!"

Now, Pom Pom is not grumpy, and he is not sad.   He is happy!

Pom Pom   friends   happy
sad   play   jump rope   football

In picture a, Pom Pom is sad. In picture b, Pom Pom is happy.

16 **Read the questions.**
Write the answers. 📖 ✏️

1 In the morning, who has Pom Pom's favorite toy?

Pom Pom's baby brother has his favorite toy.

2 At breakfast, what is Pom Pom's mommy listening to?

She is listening music .

3 At school, where are Pom Pom's friends?

They are in the playground .

4 What does Pom Pom shout at his friends?

"Don't talk to me !

17 Look and read. Write the correct names in the boxes.

Buddy   Mommy   Scout   baby brother

Pom Pom's family	Pom Pom's friends
Mommy	buddy
baby brother	scout

18 **Complete the sentences.**
Write a—e.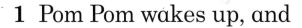

1 Pom Pom wakes up, and .... b

2 They go to school, ...

3 Pom Pom's friends say, ...

4 Pom Pom shouts ....

5 Pom Pom's friends go, ...

a and Pom Pom is sad.

b he is grumpy.

c but the sun is too hot.

d "Let's play!"

e at his friends.

19 Draw a picture of your favorite game. Then, read the questions and write the answers. 📖 ✏️

1 What is your favorite game?

race car

2 Who do you play it with?

brother

3 Where do you play it?

at home
inside

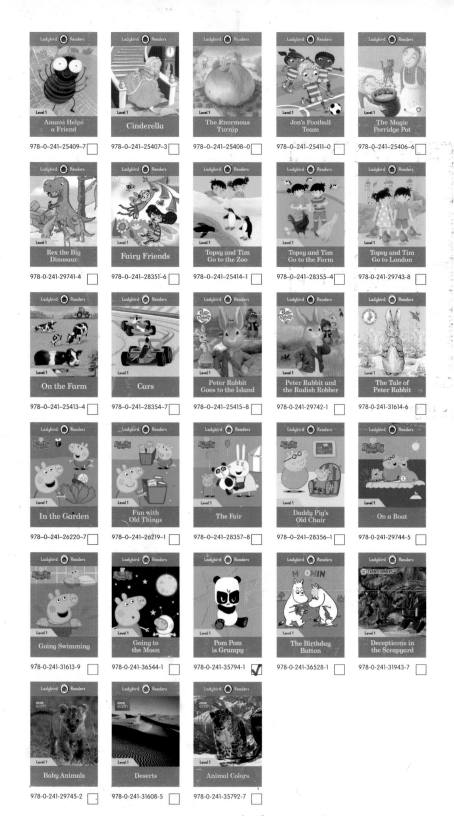

Anansi Helps a Friend	**Cinderella**	**The Enormous Turnip**	**Jon's Football Team**	**The Magic Porridge Pot**
978-0-241-25409-7	978-0-241-25407-3	978-0-241-25408-0	978-0-241-25411-0	978-0-241-25406-6
Rex the Big Dinosaur	**Fairy Friends**	**Topsy and Tim Go to the Zoo**	**Topsy and Tim Go to the Farm**	**Topsy and Tim Go to London**
978-0-241-29741-4	978-0-241-28351-6	978-0-241-25414-1	978-0-241-28355-4	978-0-241-29743-8
On the Farm	**Cars**	**Peter Rabbit Goes to the Island**	**Peter Rabbit and the Radish Robber**	**The Tale of Peter Rabbit**
978-0-241-25413-4	978-0-241-28354-7	978-0-241-25415-8	978-0-241-29742-1	978-0-241-31614-6
In the Garden	**Fun with Old Things**	**The Fair**	**Daddy Pig's Old Chair**	**On a Boat**
978-0-241-26220-7	978-0-241-26219-1	978-0-241-28357-8	978-0-241-28356-1	978-0-241-29744-5
Going Swimming	**Going to the Moon**	**Pom Pom is Grumpy**	**The Birthday Button**	**Decepticons in the Scrapyard**
978-0-241-31613-9	978-0-241-36544-1	978-0-241-35794-1 ✓	978-0-241-36528-1	978-0-241-31943-7
Baby Animals	**Deserts**	**Animal Colors**		
978-0-241-29745-2	978-0-241-31608-5	978-0-241-35792-7		

Now you're ready for Level 2!